*Special thanks to
Dylan B. and Bakken Books
for taking a chance
on a guy from Michigan!*

Hometown Hunters

The Legend of the Ghost Buck
The Hunt for Scarface
Terror on Deadwood Lake
The Boss on Redemption Road
The Day It Rained Ducks
The Lost Deer Camp

The Fishing Chronicles

Monster of Farallon Islands
The River King
The Ice Queen
The Bass Factory
The Search for Big Lou

For more books, check out:
www.lanewalkerbooks.com

Kids, always remember these three things:

Work hard.

Be nice.

Keep hunting your dreams.

-1-

My fishing line tightened, then went limp just as I was getting ready to set the hook.

Within seconds the fish hit again, but this time I was ready. I jerked towards the sky with all my strength, setting the hook. The weight of the fish pulled me back down to my cold bucket.

The fish was big—really big.

I tried to peer through the icy hole, but the water was a dark, deep blue, making it impossible to see through it.

This fish was smart, which was another good sign, because the really big ones were the cleverest.

I had learned a lot about ice fishing from years of fishing and listening to stories from anglers while working in our family's bait shop. I knew I had something special on the other end of my pole.

I let out some additional line, reducing the tension and allowing the fish to take the lure deeper. I didn't want to risk breaking the line and losing the fish.

"This could be the fish," I said, leaning over to my ten-year-old brother Mason.

"Josey, be careful! We need this fish. Mom and Dad need this fish," whispered Mason.

I knew that; I didn't need the added pressure of his saying it out loud. My hand was starting to tingle from the weight and pressure of the fish. I was athletic for a 14-year-old girl, but this fish was testing everything I had. Plus, the air was cold—bitter cold. Even with the adrenaline rushing through my body, I was still shivering. I tried to convince myself it was from the subzero winter temperature in Minnesota.

I was lying to myself. I was shaking because I knew I had something special on the other end of the line. This one fish could change everything for our family.

When I felt I had given the line enough slack, I put tension back on the line, setting the hook even deeper. This was a giant fish. *But was it her? Could it be? Was there any way that a 14-year-old girl and her 10-year-old brother could catch her?*

I wasn't sure; I didn't believe in fairy tales and legends. Luck, fate, or good fortune—call it what you want, but this type of thing just didn't happen to our family.

Whatever I had on the other end of my line was like nothing I had ever hooked before. *But was it her?*

The chances were low, beyond low—like one in a billion.

I sat in disbelief, replaying the last couple of minutes and trying to convince myself otherwise.

But I couldn't; I knew she was real. I could feel the weight of the fish and our family's troubles all on the end of my jigging pole. Christmas is a season of hope of happiness.

It had to be her…

Did I just hook the Ice Queen?

-2-

The multi-colored Christmas-themed flyer said it all:

59th Annual Ice Queen
Fishing Contest

$20,000 grand prize for state record book fish

$10,000 prize for first place

Contest ends at 8:00 p.m. on December 23

Merry Christmas and Happy Ice Queen!

Dad chuckled as he posted the flyers all over our family-owned bait shop—Baxter's Bait and Tackle. My dad was the third-generation family owner of the shop. My great-grandpa started it more than 60 years ago, and the shop became a regular fixture in Baudette, Minnesota.

Baudette is known as the Walleye Capital of the World. In fact, a huge walleye statue, affectionately named Willie the Walleye, greets visitors to our small town. More than 40 feet long, the statue has become famous and provides a perfect photo opportunity for locals and tourists alike. The fish even has a festival named after him—Willie Walleye Festival—that takes place the first week of June.

Our town is known for one thing: ice fishing. We're located 26 miles south of Lake of the Woods and have some of the best ice fishing in the world.

Lake of the Woods is the sixth largest freshwater lake in the United States, only behind the five Great Lakes. The lake is 85 miles long and 56 miles wide, covering 1,727 miles.

During the beautiful summers, our town is invaded by vacationers and tourists. Most come to fish and enjoy the rich beaches of the Lake of the Woods.

While summer is busy, the winter season is the

reason our town survives financially. Local business-es take in 75 percent of their income from December through early March. Our family bait shop opens early and closes late during the winter months.

The winters in Minnesota are brutal, with snow-storms and freezing temperatures. Once the lake freezes, it's transformed into a booming city on ice. Winter in Baudette brings ice fisherman in search of monster walleyes, the really big ones that the Lake of the Woods is known for.

And so, Lake of the Woods becomes littered with thousands of ice shanties filled with anglers dreaming of catching a trophy fish. The unique fishing camps look more like small houses. Some shanties are decked out and customized, complete with bathrooms and wireless Internet. They're comfortable enough for anyone to spend the entire winter on the ice.

Some fishermen spend weeks at a time living on the ice. Norm Fitzpatrick has the record—65 straight days on the frozen Lake of the Woods without com-ing to shore.

An abundant supply and variety of fish live in the lake, including the popular Northern pike and muskie. Still, walleyes are the main reason that so many people invade Lake of the Woods.

Not just your average fish, the walleyes in our lake are some of the biggest on the planet.

-3-

Towards the end of this December, the excitement was building throughout the entire state of Minnesota for the annual Ice Queen Fishing Tournament. Even at school, kids were talking about it. I was glad when the final bell rang, signaling the beginning of Christmas vacation.

I loved everything about Christmas and was super excited to have two weeks' free.

The school bus dropped me off as usual at the bait shop's main entrance since our house was attached at the back. I walked in and found a friendly crowd and a cheerful buzz within the shop.

I navigated through everyone and spotted my brother with his nose deep in a softcover book, reading in our designated corner of the shop. He had a fort set up under some shelving and surrounded by gear, so it was his own hidden spot to get away within the shop.

After I dropped my backpack behind the counter, I walked over to him.

"Maybe this will be the year that someone catches the Ice Queen," said Mason.

I just rolled my eyes. This is the same conversation we had every year.

"There is no Ice Queen," I said quickly, annoyed at a ten-year-old's fantasy.

Mason didn't like my response and returned to his book. I sat down in the beanbag next to him and scrolled on my cell phone for a couple of minutes.

Our bait shop survived because of the winter ice-fishing season. Dad always said that ice fishing and the Ice Queen competition were the reasons Baxter's Bait Shop was able to stay open for such a long time.

But as I got older, I knew that my parents could barely make ends meet most of the time. Lots of months, Dad was worried about paying the bills. He felt it was his Baxter family duty to keep the bait shop open.

The crowd usually started to slow down around 8:00 p.m., which was our official shop closing time. But it seemed like during ice-fishing season, the bait shop was never closed. People would pull in at all hours of the night for supplies. Dad would just smile, get up, and find them whatever they needed. He knew ice fishing in Baudette meant he was really open 24/7 this time of year.

Mason was still engulfed in his book when I heard the bell chime at the front door. I looked up to see Mr. Hathaway walking in. He was president of the Baudette Bank and Trust and had been a friend of my dad's since they were both in elementary school.

I thought it was odd that he had come to the shop, since he didn't fish. Looking closer, I saw that he was wearing a clean, pressed suit, which told me this was a professional visit. When he walked in, I noticed my dad's expression change. My dad was always a happy, positive person, but that changed when he spotted his old friend.

The two men started talking, and I noticed Dad looking in my direction. When I made eye contact, he quickly flashed his nervous smile and went back to whispering.

I knew something odd was going on. I got up and pretended to use the bathroom, walking right by both men as they talked by the cash register.

I could barely understand anything they were saying as they whispered back and forth. But I clearly made out one thing Mr. Hathaway said: "Brad, there is nothing else I can do. The bait shop will be owned by the bank at the end of the week. That is, unless you can pay the $20,000."

I quickly shut the door to the bathroom and stared in the mirror. *How could we lose the bait shop? Hadn't it paid off a long time ago?*

Then I remembered that my dad had to take out a high-interest mortgage on our house and the bait shop several years ago when my grandpa had gotten sick. His medical bills were very costly, and Grandpa had little money.

Grandpa needed special medical attention, which ended up costing a fortune, so my dad refinanced everything we owned. Two months later, Grandpa passed away.

I know Dad didn't regret helping him, and neither did I. He inherited a huge debt by doing so—a debt that now needed to be paid.

-4-

How could we lose the bait shop? It was a Baudette landmark and had been in our family for 60 years. I couldn't imagine the anxiety and stress Dad was going through.

I waited in the bathroom an extra couple of minutes. Then I heard the front door jingle again, which signaled Mr. Hathaway's departure. I tiptoed out to Mason's cubby, where he was now playing a handheld video game.

"How much money do you have?" I asked.

"Why? You ain't getting none," he quickly answered.

"How much?" I asked again, this time more sternly than the first.

"I have $150, but I was saving it for the Zbox 2000 video game system that comes out next month," he finally replied.

"Not enough," I mumbled.

"Why?" he asked again sharply.

Do I tell Mason? Everyone knows the kid is a loudmouth who struggles to keep even basic secrets. But if I didn't tell him, I knew there was no way he would lend me the money or help me. This was going to be a big job.

"I need it to enter the Ice Queen contest," I finally answered him.

"What? *You?* Come on, Josey, you aren't even an average fisherman. Plus, no one has caught the Ice Queen ever. It's all an old legend anyway!"

The Ice Queen Annual Fishing Contest was a one of a kind contest. The huge purse's grand prize money attracted a lot of attention and fishermen. Thousands descended on the Lake of the Woods with dreams of catching the next Ice Queen and claiming the $20,000 grand prize.

What is the Ice Queen? Simply put, she is the biggest walleye in Minnesota. To win the grand prize, someone has to catch a walleye that breaks the current state record book fish.

In the 60-year history of the contest, several anglers came close, but none tipped the scales enough to unseat the current state record. So far, the Ice Queen was a perfect 60-0. No one has set a new state record yet.

"A fish that size doesn't even exist, let alone in the Lake of the Woods," said Mason. He quickly added, "No one has ever even caught one over 17 pounds on the lake. Everyone chases around looking for the Ice Queen, but it's just another reason to go ice fishing."

"She's out there. She *has* to be this year." I was hoping I was right.

Mason just rolled his eyes and went back to playing his video game.

What were the chances of a 14-year-old girl breaking the 60-year drought and reeling in the new state record walleye in Minnesota? I knew my chances were slim, but it was our only option of keeping the shop.

I reached down and jerked off Mason's head-phones. He spun around quickly, glaring at me.

"Mason, listen to me! It's our only hope; we have to try something," I said.

"Our only hope for what?" he asked with a frown, starting to get a little concerned by my tone.

"We have to save the bait shop. We have to save our family's business and history. If we don't, Baxter's Bait Shop will be nothing but a memory!"

-5-

The thought of our losing the bait shop hit Mason and me hard. The idea of us two kids catching the Ice Queen seemed almost impossible. *Almost...*

We had grown up ice fishing and listening to the stories about the monster fish that lived in the Lake of the Woods. Ever since I was little, I had loved to sit in the bait shop and listen to the exciting stories people told about fishing the lake.

Dad would always say the shop made more money the week of the Ice Queen than the next three months combined. Our tiny town was flooded with ice shanties and fishermen with dreams of landing a legendary 18-pound walleye.

Mason and I didn't usually agree on much. He

was a peanut butter guy; I was more jelly. He liked sunshine, and I liked storms. But this was one thing that we both agreed was important.

That night both of us sat in the living room quietly thinking. Dad was, of course, out in the shop, and Mom was working. She taught a night class at the local community college on finance and accounting. We sat in silence as the television blared a news report about a huge incoming winter storm that was going to hammer northern Minnesota.

A snowstorm usually got us both excited because it had the potential of a snow day. There is nothing better on earth than a snow day! No school! The storm didn't matter much now since we already were on Christmas break and didn't have school.

Mason eventually broke the awkward silence. "Josey, I know who we need to talk to," he began.

"Who?" I asked. I knew what he meant. He had an idea of someone who could help us get the money we needed to save the bait shop.

"Who?" I asked again, this time louder.

Mason had this weird look on his face as if I wasn't going to like his answer.

He couldn't have been more right.

"The witch," he quietly mouthed, almost whispering.

"Winnie the Witch? Are you out of your mind?" I shouted.

I quickly added, "Winnifred Frances Moss, more commonly known as Winnie the Witch is the meanest, cruelest person in all of Minnesota—if not the world!"

She was pure evil and hated everyone. Her hair was bright white, and she had a peculiar mole on the right side of her face.

Everything about her was terrifying.

She lived on an old, dead-end dirt road and was the only house for miles. While not far from town, the unlit road bordered on an old cemetery from the early 1800s.

We had heard horror stories from kids at school about Winnie the Witch and her dog, Merlin. She was basically a loner and seldom left her house. I think I had seen her in town three times in my entire life. She never had worked or gotten married.

Merlin, her dog, was a mutt. He was half Rottweiler and half German shepherd. The dog was gigantic and looked more like a small horse.

The bigger problem was that the dog wasn't much nicer than Winnie.

-6-

"Mason, that is the best you could come up with?" I asked.

"What else, Josey, seriously? You're older and should be smarter than me. Who or what else could help us find the Ice Queen?" he asked with a frown.

I paused.

For the first time in his life, Mason was actually right. Winnie was 73 years old, and her family had a rich history in Baudette, especially when it came to the Ice Queen. There was a rumor that some of Winnie's distant family tried having her sent to a retirement home. She was thrown out of every one within 50 miles of Baudette.

She had no one and hated everyone.

If there was any secret to catching the Ice Queen, we both knew that only Winnie knew it.

Sixty-one years earlier, her grandfather, Augustus Moss, caught the current state record walleye, which weighed in at 18.3 pounds. His record still holds to this day. Before his passing, he was a celebrity around Baudette. Ten years ago, he was buried in the make-shift cemetery next to the family's homestead where Winnie lives.

Local ice fishermen had a ritual they would do the night before they started ice fishing. They would sneak to his grave and leave pickled bologna and hard-boiled eggs there for good luck. They thought any small sacrifice could lend them some luck with the Ice Queen. Of course, it never worked.

The Ice Queen competition meant a boatload of eggs and rotting bologna was put in the cemetery, and its awful smell spread around Winnie's house. The whole thing drove Winnie even more mad. She hated Baudette, the Ice Queen competition, and all the people who loved it.

Every year a brave soul tried to visit her to talk about her grandfather and maybe figure out where he had caught the Ice Queen. That's where Merlin came in—the dog would chase and bite anyone who entered the driveway.

Ice fishermen from around the country would have paid big money to sit down with her, but few dared to make it up her drive.

The rumor was that Augustus had told her, his only surviving grandchild, where he had caught the Ice Queen. Of course, everyone knew it was at a place nicknamed the Lost City, but no one had a clue where that was located. Winnie always denied knowing the location or anything about the fish. She got so sick of people asking, she basically holed up in her house.

But just like any hidden treasure, her denial just added to the mystery. If the Lost City were real, the knowledge of its location would give an angler a huge advantage.

Growing up around the bait shop, I would often hear some of the old-timers talking about the Lost

City and the gigantic walleyes that swam in its waters. Unfortunately, the bottom line was that no one ever really knew where it was.

In the late 1970s, a group of biologists from Minneapolis set out to find the Lost City. They brought the most high-tech sonar equipment, old maps, and other gadgets to patrol the Lake of the Woods. A summer of scanning and digging ended with no results. The only thing they found was an old steam engine that had been dumped into the lake in the late 1920s.

After the failed expedition, the stories became legends, and most people just wrote off the Lost City as a myth.

Could the Lost City be in the Lake of the Woods? Was there really a place where giant, record book walleyes lived? Was the Ice Queen just an old tall tale told around ice shanties and restaurants—just a good fish story passed down through the generations to keep anglers searching the icy bottoms.

Or was there more to the Lost City?

-7-

Word traveled fast all those years when Augustus Moss pulled his record-setting fish through the ice. Even back then, it didn't take long for Baudette to fill with people from all over Minnesota, hoping to catch a glimpse of the giant fish.

Baudette was also full of newspaper reporters, taking pictures and interviewing Augustus. The fish really put our small town on the map. Local businesses were thrilled as anglers traveled there and spent money on their way to fish the Lake of the Woods. The lake went from hosting a couple hundred anglers to thousands upon thousands.

Moss set off a chain of events that many of the townspeople still talk about to this day, thus beginning the Ice Queen Fishing Competition. Seeing all the added sales and tourists, the town council voted for it, and the competition started the next year.

Moss was very strategic and careful whenever he gave out any details of his famous catch. He had never indicated where he had caught the fish, just saying that it was at his shanty on the Lake of the Woods.

During the ice-fishing season, the number of ice shanties built on the lake is shocking. The lake is transformed by them. Two restaurants and a grocery store even operate full time on the ice from late November.

A crazy thing happened just days after Moss' famous catch. Moss had caught the fish in late December right before Christmas. Something mysterious and tragic happened just days afterward—a heatwave hit Minnesota. There were five straight days of temperatures above 70 degrees.

The record temperatures still hold to this day. As a result, the ice melted quickly and became dangerous and unpredictable. By the time the heat wave ended, a lot of the ice on the Lake of the Woods was thin and dangerous.

With the dangerous melting ice, anglers decided to leave and wait for colder temperatures before they returned. When the ice completely melted, hundreds of the shanties became victims of the heat wave and sank down into the waters.

Two records were broken that year. The first record was August Moss and his 18.3 pound walleye. The second was the record warm front leading into Christmas that produced the warmest temperatures on record for December in Minnesota.

To date, no one has caught an 18-pound walleye, and the temperatures have never even come close to the warm front that they experienced.

-8-

The legend of the Lost City was a story told around campfires, and when grandchildren visited their grandparents. It seemed like nothing more than a nice story told by older people. But I've heard that ten years ago, the legend was rekindled at the funeral of Augustus Moss.

The story goes that Moss was part of a special group of ice fisherman who called themselves "The Twelve." They based their group's name after the twelve disciples from the Bible.

Moss and six of the other men in the group were all local pastors. The Twelve met every Wednesday morning for breakfast at Dell's Diner on Main Street. Not a single member ever missed a Wednesday meeting. They ate breakfast, read Scripture from the Bible, and shared stories about life but mostly about ice fishing.

Besides sharing a common interest in Scripture, every member of the twelve was an ice-fishing fanatic! During the winter months, the men met early so they could enjoy a full day on the ice.

There were strict rules about joining The Twelve. In fact, it was an invitation-only club and was limited to just twelve members—no more, no less.

While the rules for application to The Twelve remained a mystery, what is known is that they were a tight group that held to their secrets and traditions. Whenever a member passed away or wanted out, their spot was quickly filled. There was a long waiting list of applicants desiring to become one of The Twelve.

What also made the group so unique was its potpourri of culture and ethnicity, comprised of members of varied colors and races. This diversity never wavered and was strengthened through the

Civil Rights Movement in the late 1950s and the early 1960s.

The Twelve were very well thought of and powerful in our town. August was one of the last of the original ones to pass. At his funeral, the only surviving original member of the twelve made a crucial mistake. Some have said that it was his old age, others guessed he said something because he was the only one left and didn't think it mattered anymore. Whatever the reason, his words cast a heavy dose of gasoline and lit a match on the concept of the Lost City.

Bill Graham was the last to speak at Augustus' funeral. Most of what he shared was about the friendship and the respect he had gained over the years for Augustus. But in the last couple minutes of his speech, he surprisingly referenced the Lost City.

The mic crackled as Bill's voice quavered, mostly due to his age and tenderness at the loss of Moss. "I still remember the day he caught the Ice Queen. The Twelve had made an oath that day to keep the location a secret. The eerie warm weather had already claimed all of our ice shanties. In the spring, we took a rowboat out, hoping to salvage some of our things. But it was too late, for all we saw was the outline of the top of our shanties and several monster walleyes swimming around them. That's when we called our spot the *Lost City*."

Bill's voice cracked again and then he went on to finish, "We made a solemn vow never to fish there again or mention the location of the Lost City. We decided to hold it sacred to preserve The Twelve and Augustus' record book catch. I have always kept that promise, and now with Augustus Moss' death, the Lost City will stay that way forever!"

A murmur spread inside the church. Several local fishermen got up and shyly slipped out of the church. While this may seem rude to some, people have to understand the importance of ice fishing in Baudette.

My dad had said that the Lost City was suddenly recognized as being real as it is to this day. That meant if there was a hidden spot with giant walleyes, there could be more state record book fish just waiting to be caught there.

And someone would have the chance to have his or her name written in the record books, plus a $20,000 cash prize!

-9-

After all these years, no one had ever found the Lost City or caught the next Ice Queen. Not even biologists with special high-tech equipment could find any trace of the Lost City. *How in the world would two kids from Baudette catch the next Ice Queen?*

Our house was filled with excitement. Of all the weeks to have a challenge of this type, it had to be this week. Mom was frantically working on plans for our family's annual Christmas party and dinner.

On December 23rd, we always hosted the Baxter Christmas party after the conclusion of the Ice Queen competition. Family from all over the world came back to Baudette to enjoy the Ice Queen festivities and celebrate Christmas. We usually had over

100 people at the party, and Mom did a majority of the cooking. To make this time crazier, the bait shop was open from 6:00 a.m. until 8:00 p.m. due to all the anglers in town for the Ice Queen competition.

The busyness of the holiday season did hold some major advantages for Mason and me this year—it would give us a chance to get out of the house to search for the Ice Queen.

We usually spent a lot of time in our rooms. Mason played video games while I was zoned out on my cell phone. Dad always hired our older cousin Ryan full-time during the Christmas break, so there wasn't a ton to do around the bait shop, but we chipped in when he needed us. Ryan was a business major and home on break from Concordia University in St. Paul.

It was Sunday night, and we only had six nights until the end of the Ice Queen Competition. Six nights to save the bait shop.

After dinner, I motioned for Mason to meet me in my room. "What?" he asked.

What a boy! He was so clueless; it was two days

ago that I had told him that we needed to come up with a plan to save the bait shop. Now he was acting like I was bothering him.

"Mason, now is not the time!" I snapped.

He could tell by my voice that I was serious. I was still bigger and meaner than he was, so his body language changed quickly. He looked up and was serious now, waiting for me to finish.

I added, "We need to start the plan. We need to find the Lost City."

"How? Huh, smarty pants? How can we do the impossible? Scientists with radar equipment couldn't even do it," Mason replied with a frown.

"Well, we have to do something!" I shot back. "What's your plan? Oh wait, let me guess, all you care about are your stupid video games."

Mason jumped up. "One, they aren't stupid. And two, yeah I plan on saving the bait shop. I got this. I'm going to win the *Gauntlet* Christmas Challenge that pays out $10,000. It ends Thursday night at midnight, so don't worry."

Gauntlet was the most popular, role-playing video game on the planet. In the game, the player tries to find hidden treasures while saving the beautiful princess. It took place in medieval times. I think Mason liked the idea of carrying an ax and shooting a bow while saving the princess.

"Really? And how many people are registered for this gaming challenge?" I asked.

"Over a million worldwide," he proudly said.

If the idea of finding the Lost City was a crazy idea, Mason's plan of winning a worldwide video game tournament was nearly impossible. Mason wasn't even that good at video games. It was weird that he could solve really complex puzzles and find hidden things, but battling and gameplay wasn't his foray.

No, I was sure that *Gauntlet* wasn't going to our means of saving the bait shop. It was time to put Plan B into effect. It was time to do some mystery solving. It was time to find the Lost City.

And it was time to catch the next Ice Queen.

-10-

My plan sounded simple enough to me. We were going to go over to Winnie's house and win her over with our impeccable charm and Christmas spirit.

I looked out the window and saw fresh snow falling and the neighbors' Christmas lights coloring the horizon.

Why not? Isn't Christmas a season of hope?

"Josey, we got only six days to do this?" questioned Mason. He quickly added, "Doesn't give us much time. So when are we starting?"

"Good decision, Mason. It has to be tonight!"

"Tonight?" Mason whispered. It seemed like the fearless video game warrior thought he had more time to get out of it.

We went out to the kitchen and found that Mom had finished up the dishes.

"Mom, Mason and I are going to head downtown to the ice rink and do some skating."

"Okay, honey, be safe and take care of your brother," Mom replied. She was decorating now, trying to make the house look perfect for Friday's party.

On the way out of the house, we grabbed our ice skates. The skating rink was only a couple blocks from our house but instead of turning left out of the driveway, I turned right, heading out of town.

"Josey, the rink is the other way."

"We're going to make a little detour on our way."

"Oh, okay. Where are we going? There's nothing that way but dead ends."

"We're going to visit an elderly woman who needs a little Christmas cheer," I began.

"Huh?" Mason replied with a frown.

"Think about it, Mason, where do you think we're going?" I asked in a stern voice.

"Oh, no! No! No! No! I'm not going to the witch's

house tonight! Why in the world would we go there ever—let alone in the dark?" asked Mason, his voice rising higher than usual.

I grabbed his arm and pulled him down the street. It didn't take us long before we were out of town. We turned one last time as we rounded the corner of Marble Way Lane. The view behind us looked like something out of a magazine. Bright lights, colorful Christmas decorations, and fresh, powdery snow highlighted the incredible view.

"What are you doing?" asked Mason.

"Taking one last glance, just in case it's our last," I said in a spooky voice.

"Are you serious?" asked Mason shakily.

"Of course not! I wanted to make sure I have a positive picture in my mind when I go to knock on the witch's house," I reassured him.

Mason nodded, and we started walking. Winnie lived a quarter mile down on Marble Way Lane.

After a quick ten-minute walk, a soft, white glow appeared through the snow. It resembled the leftover ashes of a campfire, barely burning with just a glimpse of light.

As we rounded the corner and started up the driveway, the snow came down harder, making it hard to see.

"What's that?" I asked.

"I don't know; I can't see a thing," Mason said, shielding his eyes from the snow.

"No, listen," I whispered.

A low growl sounded in front of us, and a big, dark shadow emerged from the front porch.

-11-

Merlin took two large bounds down the porch steps and hit the ground running full speed towards us. The old dog had more energy than I had expected.

Mason turned to run but slipped on the slick, fresh snow. I dropped my backpack to the ground quickly and started rummaging through it. I could hear Merlin's paws thundering as they hit the snow.

I managed to grasp a large T-bone steak I had borrowed from the refrigerator and flung it into the nearby bushes.

Just as Merlin was about to pounce on Mason, the dog turned and darted into the weeds after the fresh slab of meat.

"Hurry, Mason, that steak will only last a couple

of minutes. This is our only chance," I said as I started jogging to the witch's door.

Mason followed, panting and out of breath. The thought of being supper for Merlin terrified him. The steps creaked like in a horror film as we walked towards the front door. There was no doorbell, so I knocked as hard as I could on the big oak door.

"Listen, Mason, go with me on this. When she opens the door, do exactly what I do," I told him.

"Okay," Mason said, wheezing from our run.

This time I knocked and kicked the door at the same time. A loud, scratchy voice echoed through the door. "Go home! I ain't buying nothing!"

Wow, I could see why they called her a witch. Her voice was raspy and coarse. It reminded me of fingernails dragging on a chalkboard.

I knocked again. This time I heard footsteps and a bolt unlocking. A small sliver of light escaped through the opening as we stood on the cold, barren porch. A mysterious eye appeared in the crack, staring at both of us.

There was moment of short, awkward silence. Without saying a word, I began singing. "We wish you a merry Christmas! We wish you a merry Christmas and a happy new year," I bellowed, looking at Mason to join in. At first, he didn't get the cue, but when he did, he quickly joined in.

We sang through the song twice before Winnie said something. "Be quiet! You two are awful singers!" she shouted at us.

"We're just trying to spread some Christmas cheer," I explained.

"Not interested; go home," Winnie barked as she attempted to slam the door on us. I managed to sneak my boot in before it shut.

This is not going as I planned. I knew she was rough, but who wouldn't want two kids singing Christmas carols on your front porch?

Suddenly I felt a hand on my back as Mason pushed past me and through the door. "What's that sound?" he asked, pushing the door open.

Winnie just backed up in shock as Mason entered

her house. No one usually made it past Merlin, and no one had ever made it into the house!

Did he hear the bloody moans of one of the witch's unfortunate victims? What in the world was Mason doing? What had he heard?

-12-

I followed closely, holding the back of his shirt as Mason wandered through the house towards the noise. It appeared to be coming from what looked like Winnie's living room.

"Are you playing *Gauntlet*?" he asked with a smile.

To my shock, Winnie's living room looked like a video gamer's paradise.

There were multiple televisions with video games streaming. A large 80-inch flat-screen monitor hung above a gaming desk and chair in the middle of the room. There, large as life, was the same game that Mason was obsessed with.

"I'm stuck at the Vice-Lord in Level 33 on Lost Souls' Island," she explained.

"Yeah, that's a tough level. It took me forever to figure out how to beat him," Mason admitted.

What? I never imagined someone in their 70s would be a gamer, especially Winnie. But the evidence was right there in front of me—in high-definition.

The two bantered back and forth about graphics and weapons for a couple of minutes.

"Do you know how to beat him?" Winnie asked hopefully.

"Yeah, there is a trick, it took me weeks to figure it out. You have to—" said Mason. Just as he was about to finish, I grabbed his arm and interrupted their conversation.

"Wait, just a second!" I demanded.

Winnie and Mason both turned, annoyed that I had stopped their video game party.

"Winnie, I'm sure Mason would love to help you beat the…whatever it is you're trying to beat. But we came here for some information as well. Maybe we can do a little trade," I offered.

"A trade? What do you want from me?" she grumbled.

"The same thing you want from Mason—just a little information to solve a problem."

"And you will tell me how to beat the ViceLord?" she asked my brother.

"Yep, every detail, plus there's a hidden gold lunar gem in this level," Mason added.

"A gold lunar gem? No way! I've searched everywhere for one!" she exclaimed.

I grinned.

It was simple—a trade. She had information that I wanted; Mason had information that she wanted.

I took a deep breath and blurted out quickly, "Please tell us the location of the Lost City."

Winnie's expression changed, and she started to laugh. She was laughing so hard that tears began running down her cheeks.

"You two think I know? People are so dumb! They've offered me thousands of dollars if I told them. I could care less about any stupid fish. I would have taken the money years ago if I had known where it was," she said loudly. "I don't have a clue about the location of the Lost City. Frankly, I'm sick and tired of people asking. But you need to keep up your end of the deal if I give you any information," she said sternly.

"Not quite yet," I responded. "If you don't know where the city is, can you tell us of any hints or clues that your Grandpa Augustus left in this house?"

She sat for a minute and walked over towards the fireplace. She leaned on the banister and stoked the coals in the fire.

"Yeah, I can tell you the only thing that I do know. He told me this old picture would be the key to finding the Lost City," she said as she pointed to an old photograph. "Sadly, I've stared at that picture for the past fifty years, and I see no clues! Nothing!" She sighed sadly.

I had to make a choice. She had given me a clue—something to help continue the search. Plus, I still wasn't convinced of what she was going to do to us.

"Go ahead, Mason, tell Winnie how to beat the level."

The pair quickly forgot about me as Winnie grabbed the video game remote control, navigating towards the Vice-Lord.

While Mason and Winnie were busy figuring out *Gauntlet*, I walked over to examine the picture for myself.

-13-

"Has this picture always hung in this exact location?" I asked her.

"Yep, always," replied Winnie without ever taking her eyes off the video screen.

The photograph was an old, faded, black-and-white portrait, with yellow stains from age. The first thing that caught my eye was the giant walleye. I had never seen a walleye this size! The fish was so big it almost looked fake.

Augustus Moss was standing stiffly, holding the walleye in his right hand. As I examined the picture, everything looked fairly normal. I took the photo down and scanned every inch of it. Then I saw something odd, and I was surprised that I hadn't seen it before. Augustus' left hand was clinched with his index and middle fingers pointing straight down.

Two?

My mind starting reeling with ideas. Maybe the number two had a special meaning to the Moss family.

"Winnie, what did you think when I said the number two?" I asked.

No response. So I asked again, this time a little louder.

"Two? You really want me to tell you?" she asked, looking down at Mason and winking at him. They both laughed as he quickly picked up on her bathroom reference humor.

"No, I mean in your family. Does the number two mean anything?'

"Nope, nothing. My dad had one son, and I am his only grandchild," she explained.

The two played on, and within minutes, Mason had helped her beat the level she had been stuck on for weeks, unlocking uncharted levels on *Gauntlet*.

I replaced the picture where it belong above the

mantel. I went and sat on the couch, facing the fireplace. I stared at the picture for the next ten minutes with a million ideas running through my mind on the possibilities of what the number two could mean to finding the Lost City.

This is stupid, I told myself. *What am I doing here wasting time listening to some old lady and my geeky brother play a stupid video game? What was I thinking?*

I was desperate, but I was also beginning to realize this whole thing was probably just a giant goose chase. Besides Mason's making a new friend and realizing that Winnie was actually a really cool old lady, I had wasted one of Mom's prize steaks. Tonight had become another night closer to our losing the bait shop.

I took a deep breath as the lights of the video game flashed behind me. The parade of bold colors reminded me of the Fourth of July. The bright lights reflected on the beige wall behind me and cast a warm glow.

Then I saw something.

A brilliant flash of red from the game silhouetted on the picture of Augustus Moss. The bright color highlighted the photograph so brightly that more of the actual picture was revealed.

I had found what I was missing, and it was right in front of my eyes—hidden in plain sight the entire time!

-14-

The idea of something hidden in plain sight is interesting. When Mason and I were younger, one of my best hiding spots was in the closet right by his bedroom. For whatever reason, he was so excited to find me that he often just walked right past me.

This picture had something hidden the whole time that only became obvious when the bright-red light cast by the video game shone on it. I walked up and removed the picture once again.

"Winnie, do you have a flashlight handy?"

"Yeah, top drawer in the kitchen," she bellowed. I could have asked her for anything; she didn't care. She was so engrossed in the video game.

I found the flashlight and then grabbed the photo and went into the small half bathroom located down a narrow hallway next to the kitchen. As I walked in, I flipped off the light switch.

I took the flashlight and focused the beam directly on Augustus' right hand. There was substantial staining and fading, almost giving the hand a smeared "blob" appearance.

But when I isolated the light, I could make out each finger. Moss was holding the fish with his thumb and index finger. The other three fingers were pointing straight down. I slowly spun the picture upside down, inverting the image and there it was clear as could be.

Augustus Moss' fingers spelled out the number twenty-three. *Twenty-three?* I walked back through the hallway and the kitchen into the living room. I carefully hung the picture back above the mantel, making sure everything was straight and level.

"Winnie, how about the number twenty-three?" I asked.

She stopped playing the video game. "Yeah, that number does mean something to me," she said after a minute.

Mason and I both stared, locked into her every word. She could be holding the last missing key to finding the Lost City.

"Twenty-three? Now that you mention it, that number does mean something to me. It reminds me of the 23 million times I've been asked stupid question about that fish," she said and grinned.

"Forget it," I said. It seemed pointless. We had gotten the only clue we could, and Winnie would be no further help. It seemed Winnie knew nothing about the Lost City or giant walleyes.

But *Gauntlet*—that was a different story.

"Mason, we need to get heading back. Mom and Dad are going to start to wonder where we are."

Mason got up reluctantly, and we headed out the door. Winnie kept playing the video game, just grunting when we said goodbye.

Just as we were about to close the door, she

yelled, "Add my online gamer name next time you're online: icequeen56623!"

As the front door slammed shut, I asked, "Mason, what does that mean?"

"Now we can play *Gauntlet* together online," explained Mason. I recognized 56623—it was the zip code for Baudette.

I was relieved to see it had stopped snowing. Our walk home went fast, and I made sure we made a detour by the ice-skating rink. I didn't want to lie to my parents. I knew we had to figure out what Augustus was trying to tell us. The number twenty-three didn't make any sense, but he had gone out of his way to do it in the photo.

Even in all the excitement of landing the record book fish, he still managed to conceal his secret. As we neared the downtown, we were greeted with festive Christmas music. During the Ice Queen, downtown Baudette took on the appearance of the North Pole. It was decorated in Christmas lights and inflatable decorations while Christmas music blared through all the speakers. A bunch of fun events and contests were held all week.

There was something magical about the Christmas season, the snow and the tradition of the Ice Queen fishing contest. It made Baudette a special place; it made my home special.

Even with the stress of possibly losing the bait shop, the Christmas season was still a season of hope.

I just had to figure out what the number twenty-three meant.

- 15 -

Mason went into the house to ask Mom if he could add Winnie online so they could play *Gauntlet* together. My parents had a rule that he could only add his friends while anyone who was older had to get approved by my parents first. We knew the dangers of online gaming for kids and took it very seriously. I went behind the counter to talk to Dad.

"You know a lot about ice fishing, Dad. Are numbers ever used for anything related to it?"

"Josey, that's an odd question. Why do you ask?"

"I'm just wondering. You know, like with lures, or bait, or maybe a location of where to fish. Like maybe something about the number twenty-three. Would that mean anything to you?"

"Oh, okay, a lot of fisherman use GPS coordinates to save their locations where the fish are baiting. But those aren't double digit numbers, they're much larger. There are different spoon sizes of lures, but no lures go up that high in number. I can't think of anything that relates to ice fishing that would have the number twenty-three," said Dad.

There wasn't much about ice fishing my dad wasn't an expert on. He had grown up on the ice and knew every type of line, lure, or anything associated with ice fishing.

"Okay! Thanks, Dad. I love you. Goodnight."

Part of my soul wanted to tell Dad that I knew about the shop and was trying to help find a solution to save it. But I didn't. I told myself it was better if Dad had no idea that I had overheard the conversation with the bank. I didn't want to burden or worry him even more than he already was.

Mason and I had made a pact to not tell anyone about it—not a single person. He promised on his video game system, and I did on my cell phone.

It seemed like a fair deal. That night I had trouble sleeping. I knew the next morning would mean we only had five days left to solve the mystery of the Lost City and catch the Ice Queen.

The sky darkened and our neighbor's electric timer went on, releasing power to their Christmas lights.

I went up to my bedroom and got ready for bed. It was now midnight as I struggled to sleep. I had no more leads, no new ideas. If I didn't find out what old Augustus was trying to tell us, our bait shop would be history.

-16-

Monday morning came fast. I was exhausted from the stress of everything so I woke up a little after 10:00 and ate breakfast. Mom had a lengthy list for both Mason and me to do around the house in preparation for the Christmas party Friday night.

Our family party was usually the culminating event of the year. Most of the Baxter side of our family returned from all over the world to celebrate Christmas and join in the Ice Queen competition. The mood around our house was anything but festive. Mom would always get antsy and short with us this week. Most of the party details fell on her, and she was overwhelmed with the set-up and involved with most of the cooking for the more than hundred people who were coming to the party. There was something different this year.

Mom had even more anxiety because of the financial problems with the bait shop. She knew how much it meant to my dad and the entire Baxter family. It was breaking her heart watching him frantically scrambling around doing everything he could to save the bait shop.

To Dad's credit, he never let on. He smiled at every customer, ran incredible deals and discounts, and acted like everything was perfect at the bait shop. The register clanked and dinged all week. But even if Dad had the best week of his life, we were still going to come up terribly short to pay off the bank. He had other bills to pay, so I knew that we had to come up with a minimum of $20,000 to save the shop.

Dad knew it but wanted to enjoy one last season as the best bait shop in Baudette. If this was his last Ice Queen event, he might as well make sure everyone enjoyed it.

By late afternoon, I was still looking for a solution. The shop was crazy busy all day. I spent most of the time scooping out minnows and restocking all the lures. The shelves were getting ready to be restocked by late afternoon when I heard the shop bell chime.

Mr. O'Connor, the head of the Baudette Historical Society, strolled in carrying a box.

"Can I help you with something, Mr. O'Connor?" I asked.

"Hello, Josey! I just found a bunch of old icefishing memorabilia in the museum basement. Our staff has already gone through it and kept anything valuable. I wanted to see if your dad wanted any of it before we threw it away," he said.

I glanced over at Dad, who was swamped with customers looking at gas-powered ice augers.

"I'll take it for him, Mr. O'Connor." I reached for the box. He nodded and wished me a Merry Christmas and a happy Ice Queen—the common phrase around Baudette the entire week.

"Thanks, you too." I smiled.

I grabbed the box and was surprised by how light it was. I scanned inside and found some old maps, a scroll-looking thing, a couple of Baudette history books, and what looked like an antique flyer advertising some type of farm implement sale. Moving around the counter, I put the box by the copy machine near where Mason and I hung out.

On the outside, the town and the bait shop seemed like their normal, festive self. Sometimes things can look and feel a certain way, but on the inside, be the total opposite.

-17-

Tuesday…only four days left until the end of the Ice Queen competition and the possible end of the Baxter Bait Shop.

If the original task had seemed impossible, every second that ticked closer to Friday's 8:00 p.m. deadline made it even less possible.

Mason walked into my room.

"I had a great idea this morning, Josey. Maybe we should go back to Winnie's for more clues," he suggested.

Really? We already knew there were no more clues because Winnie had told us what little she knew. I figured this was just his attempt to go back to play video games with her.

"We already know everything from Winnie," I reminded him.

"Well, I don't want to burst your bubble, Josey, but I'm not going to win that *Gauntlet* tournament. I got knocked out late last night. I did terrible; Winnie lasted longer than I did."

I had to laugh. The whole time Mason was thinking that he actually had a chance to win the tournament. I wrote off that idea the second he had mentioned it.

"Mason, that's okay," I said softly, not wanting to burst his bubble, but I had no idea he had even entered the contest.

During the week of the Ice Queen competition, the mayor always ran an updated leader board downtown on stage. A huge board hung there—almost like at a golf match. People flocked downtown to see who was leading and how big the fish was on top of the board. It was a tradition and something we checked every night.

It was a Baudette holiday tradition for cars to cruise town to check out the board and the Christmas lights.

Dad had checked it the night before and commented on how many big walleyes were already listed. Local legend Tim Silverman had the largest one that weighed just over 14 pounds. Even though it wasn't close to the state record, the biggest fish at the end of the week would still bring a $10,000 cash prize to the lucky fisherman.

To say the contest was heated and competitive would be an understatement. Besides the prize money and the possibility of winning the $20,000 grand prize, the ego of every ice fisherman was on the line. It was a huge deal to be declared the first- place winner of the Ice Queen Competition.

All the really gigantic walleyes were females. Usually females hunted together, and that was what made the Lost City so intriguing. Supposedly, The Twelve had told people that they had found a secret spot of gigantic, female walleyes when they caught the original Ice Queen. Their secret spot only doubled in legend when all the ice shanties sank, actually making it a lost city, sinking their secret to the bottom of the lake.

-18-

It was hard to believe it was already Wednesday. The stress was starting to show at our house at an even higher level. Mom was constantly busy with the preparation for the family Christmas party.

Dad was staying busy too. He was doing everything he could to save the bait shop. I knew what was happening and didn't want to bring it up. Last night he had sold our two four-wheelers. Mason was upset at first, but then he too realized what was going on. Dad didn't go into much of an explanation; he just said we didn't use them very much. But Mason and I knew the real reason.

Dad only cleared $3,000 by selling the ATVs. I had overheard him on the phone that morning telling the bank he needed more time, or he was going to be about $17,000 short. The bank didn't care. They wanted their money or the bait shop.

Dad hung up the phone and gave us some jobs to do to help around the shop. The bait shop started getting really busy around 11:00 a.m.

Anglers were telling mighty stories of the walleyes they were catching on the Lake of the Woods. Overall, the season was a huge success, and the fish were biting everywhere.

I was sure if we asked friends or customers for help, someone would have stepped up with the money to help save the shop. I also knew Dad was too proud to ask for help, and I was too ashamed to ask him why.

We could hardly keep the shelves full, especially of Swedish Pimples. This lure was invented in Sweden, and the name means "to jig." The lure is made with a metallic-colored spoon and a treble hook.

Jigging was the most common way of ice fishing for walleyes, and the Swedish Pimples were our most popular lures. We carried every color imaginable. The walleye bite proved to be even better when a multi-colored Swedish Pimple was used.

Baxter's Bait Shop was swamped the entire day on Wednesday. We actually sold out of several items, including Swedish Pimples. Dad was expecting a shipment later that night.

The shop started to slow down around 8:00 p.m. I didn't think I could listen to another ice-fishing story or look at another picture of someone holding up a huge walleye.

Dad walked over to Mason and me, trying to make small talk. "What a day! Hey, I was thinking that you guys haven't given me your Christmas lists yet this year."

The Baxter family Christmas list was something Mason and I looked forward to every year. We usually started making it around Thanksgiving. Mom and Dad always tried to get us at least one thing on it. We always had fun making the list and dreaming of unwrapping something cool on Christmas morning.

Mason and I sat silent for a couple seconds.

"Dad, we've been so busy with school and the shop. We'll give them to you once the Ice Queen and Christmas party are over," I finally said.

"Oh, okay," Dad said, quietly disappointed. I could tell he knew we knew something, but he didn't want to say it aloud.

How could we make a Christmas list if we were going to lose the shop? I was proud of Mason for understanding and not making it a big deal. Not a lot of kids would handle it that way. I smiled at him.

"What?" Mason asked.

"Nothing. I'm just happy you kept your mouth closed."

Mason shrugged like it was no big deal.

I grabbed a box of lures to restock the south wall. Mason got the hint and grabbed a box too. We walked over and began placing multi-colored spoons on the wall.

"What's this?" Mason questioned, glancing into the old box from the Baudette Museum.

-19-

"Looks like an old picture of downtown Baudette. Take that box to the trash," I said.

I continued restocking while Mason went to the back to dump the contents in a large garbage container.

"Josey! Josey! Come here," Mason cried out excitedly from across the room.

I rolled my eyes. I didn't have time to look at a bunch of junky history stuff about Baudette.

Mason's eyes were the size of Christmas bulbs, and I could tell he had found something special. I glanced over his shoulder into the box of junk. At first, I just saw some old photographs and flyers. There were also some old, worn-out books I'd already

---

examined. I scanned the box, and when I looked up, Mason was holding something.

"What's that?" I asked.

"Some type of map book or something," he said. I grabbed the aged binding and turned it over on the counter.

"Looks like an old map of Lake of the Woods. Mason, we don't have time for this," I reminded him.

"Flip to the back of the book," he said. Mason was obsessed with maps and such. That was part of the reason he loved *Gauntlet* so much. He liked to study them and memorize their locations.

I flipped towards the back of the book as pieces of each page crumbled and fell off.

The musty smell was overwhelming, and I was just about to throw the book at Mason when I saw it. The last page of the book had a plot map of the Lake of the Woods. I had seen a lot of maps of the lake. Our local restaurants had maps, and our school gave us maps. Dad even had several pinned on the wall of the bait shop. But I had never seen a map like this.

This map was broken up, illustrated, and hand-painted. Another more fascinating difference with this map was that there was a number grid overlaying the entire lake.

When I saw this feature, I froze, and the hair on the back of my neck stood straight up. Within seconds I had locked in on the number twenty-three!

-20-

This was the first and only time I had ever seen a map that had a number grid overlaid on it. Every square was about two inches by two inches and had a bold number on it.

"That can't be right!" Mason blurted out.

At first I didn't hear him, still in shock over the hidden clue that we had in the shop the entire week.

"That can't be right!" he repeated, pointing at number twenty-three. "That's west by Zippel Bay. Everyone knows it's shallow, and no fish are there. No way that's where the Lost City is!"

I stared at the map and saw that everything else on it, while old and dated, was 100 percent accurate. We were focusing on a spot that no one ever fished because they never caught anything there. It was more of a beach for swimming in the summer. In fact, a large part of number twenty-three was covered by land. The biggest walleyes were always caught way east of Zippel Bay, a mile north of the shore, near Pine Island.

"We need to get to Zippel Bay State Park," I said after staring at the map for a few minutes. "I really think that's where the Ice Queen lives."

"Zippel Bay State Park? Josey, there aren't even fish there."

"It's our only clue," I insisted. "Grab a couple Swedish Pimples—a coral-colored and a pink one. I'll go out to the garage and get the poles and sled ready."

We had several plastic ice-fishing sleds that were kept loaded with poles, buckets, and ice scoopers. We also had several gas ice augers to choose from that fit perfectly in the sled.

"Josey, we have one major problem. How are we going to get there? We can't drive, and it's way too far to walk," Mason reminded me.

The drive from Baudette to Zippel Bay State Park was about 20 miles.

"We can't ask Mom or Dad right now, that wouldn't be right especially with the Christmas party tomorrow," I said.

"I know who can take us to the Lost City!" Mason cried out and got out his cell phone.

-21-

I rushed to the garage and tugged the loaded sled into the driveway. I pushed it off to the side and into the yard.

Our front driveway served as an entrance for the bait shop and was filled up with customers. I peeked my head through the back door.

"Mom, Mason and I are going fishing for a bit. We'll be back later," I said.

Mom stopped long enough to give me the thumbs up and went back to cleaning. That would at least cover our tracks; she couldn't get too mad since I did tell her what we were doing.

Mason bounded down the back steps, and the two of us stood waiting at the end of the driveway.

The sun was just going down behind our house.

Who did he call? I *heard* who it was before I *saw* who it was.

A loud banging sound was coming down our road. I peered through the window to see a two-toned, wood-paneled station wagon turn into our driveway. The car had seen better days, but at least it was a ride.

To my surprise, a wrinkled lady with a raggedy Minnesota Twins hat was sitting in the driver's seat.

"Winnie, you're taking us to Zippel Bay?"

"Who in the world did you expect? Santa Claus?" she said in her old, scratchy voice.

More like the Grinch, I thought. I put on a fake smile and climbed in. At least we had a ride.

I later learned that Winnie and Mason had stayed close after our first encounter, teaming up every night to play *Gauntlet*. That crazy video game was able to connect two unlikely people by giving them a passion to share.

"Mason told me all about your silly numbered

map. I think you're loonier than me, but I didn't have anything else to do," she explained.

Winnie seemed to add to the stress of the event and was a lot to handle at times. Her voice reminded me of the sound that skates make when scratching fresh ice.

"At least it's something," I said, almost as if to reassure myself and not Winnie. We had one long shot left.

-22-

The 30-minute drive to Zippel Bay felt like 100 hours. Winnie kept the speedometer at 45 mph. I didn't want to complain, but her slow driving and the smell of the gasoline from the ice auger in the back was starting to make me carsick.

Every bump we hit just made it worse. Mason and Winnie seemed to be enjoying themselves. They chatted the entire time. I just sat in the back and stared out the window. This was our one shot, and we were going after it. When we finally pulled into the park, the sun was going down on the ice.

The orange glare from the setting sun reflected on the ice, creating a gorgeous backdrop and almost giving the impression the ice was on fire. I scanned the horizon and didn't see a single shanty or anyone fishing.

I wasn't surprised. Everyone knew the big fish stayed around the drop-offs near the large islands scattered throughout Lake of the Woods.

"This place stinks," Winnie said as she scanned the parking lot. There wasn't a single vehicle there. Winnie decided to stay in the car and read a gamer magazine.

I took a deep breath and tried my best to ignore her. Mason and I unloaded the sled and set the ice auger on top of the equipment. It took both of us heaving with all our strength to pull it the fifty yards through the deep snow until we hit the ice. Once we hit the frozen water, the sled glided naturally along. The snow from the night before was fresh and crisp. The crunchy sound of our footsteps reminded me of the Christmas song "Up on the Housetop."

Mason and I weren't reindeer, but we were hoping to deliver a gift to our family. I laughed. We were kind of like little Christmas elves on a Christmas mission.

"Now what?" Mason asked.

"I'm not sure," I said, pulling out the numbered plot map.

When we looked closely at the map, we saw the numbering was specific enough to give us a general location of number twenty-three. It seemed to stretch for a quarter mile or so. It was not a huge section. A part of number twenty-three covered some land and small rivers and jetties that went inland.

"Let's leave the sled, take the ice auger, and start making random holes every twenty feet. We need to find a deep water hole or pocket. That's where the Lost City will be," I told him.

While it sounded easy, it wasn't. I fired up the auger, and it made a loud roar. We started ripping through the thick ice.

With every hole, more disappointment flooded

in. We'd make a hole, drop onto our bellies, and peer into the water, only to continually spot the bottom of the lake.

This area was way too shallow for any fish, let alone monster walleye.

"We knew this was too shallow! This is a waste of time," Mason shouted over at me.

I turned and looked back towards the car and saw holes everywhere, making the ice look like a giant piece of Swiss cheese. I reexamined the map, and it looked like we had covered the plotted number twenty-three pretty well. There wasn't any water deep enough for walleyes. This place was just what we initially thought it was—a beach and a shallow one at that.

By now, the moon and stars had broken through the darkness. I looked towards the sky and exhaled; my breath rose and hung in the air.

We loaded the auger in the sled, feeling totally defeated, and walked back into the park at Zippel Bay.

No fish, no leads, no hope, and soon to be, no bait shop.

The contest would end tomorrow, and our only lead was officially dead.

-23-

The ride home seemed to go by much faster. We had been on the ice for about two hours, and Mason and I were both cold and disappointed. Winnie had stayed in the car and played some video game on Mason's cell phone.

"I could have told you this area is no good, but you two wouldn't have listened to an old witch. No one listens to me, but I'm used to it," Winnie said sadly.

By now, I had grown sick of Winnie's constant negativity and sarcasm. I had already asked her a hundred times for any help or hints in finding the Lost City, but she had given us none.

"It was worth a shot. At least now we know we did

everything we could to save the bait shop," I snapped back.

"Lose the bait shop? What are you talking about?" Winnie demanded with a frown.

I went on to explain the real reason we desperately needed to catch the Ice Queen and win the fishing contest. She listened, but her expression didn't change much. After I had finished, I felt some relief telling an adult about our family's financial situation.

What did it matter anyway? Tomorrow night was game over for the Baxter's Bait Shop.

Most kids are filled with so much excitement and anticipation they can hardly sleep on Christmas. Dreams of ripping through gift wrapping and opening gifts fill their minds. Not me—not this year. I was going to go to bed, knowing we didn't come through for Dad and the bait shop.

I figured Dad was going to tell everyone at the party that he had lost the bait shop. It would be weighing heavily on him, and even though it was a party, it was the only time most of our extended family was together in one spot.

Winnie slowly pulled into our driveway. We thanked her, and she gave a half-hearted wave and kept her eyes forward.

The bait shop was still open, which meant Dad couldn't tell people to leave. Often, customers would stay late, telling stories and talking about fishing. I walked in and waved to Dad to let him know we were home. He waved back but probably didn't even know we had been gone.

I walked through the bait shop and heard someone telling Dad about a 16.5-pound walleye he had caught near Snake Island. The angler was currently in first place and was confident he would win the $10,000 first place prize.

I went into the house and straight to my bedroom. I could hear Mason's video game next door, and his loud voice talking to someone. I knew he was talking to Winnie and could tell by the music they were playing *Gauntlet*.

I was exhausted and fell into a deep sleep with the battle sounds of swords and axes dancing in my head.

I wasn't sleeping long when I was startled awake by the sound of my door being flung open and hitting the wall. Mason was standing at the end of my bed, waving his arms.

"Josey, I think I know where the Lost City is!" he cried out.

-24-

My heart raced; it took me a couple seconds to get myself together. I glanced at my clock and saw I had been sleeping a little over an hour.

I asked, "What? Where? How?"

"Where's the map? I think I might have something." Mason was all smiles now.

I scrambled over to my backpack and pulled out the numbered plot map.

"See, see, ri-ri-right th-th-there! Th-th-that's it!" he said, stuttering with excitement.

"What? Mason, you're pointing at the beach," I said confused.

"No—look closer," he directed me. I pulled the map close to my eyes and could see a little blue dot on the map. A small stream connected a large pond inland off the coast of the Lake of the Woods.

"So what? There are thousands of these little pockets of water on the map. Most of them are gone or have eroded," I said annoyed.

Mason began explaining, "Winnie and I were trying to beat the Atlantis level in *Gauntlet*. It's totally underwater and hard to beat. But anyway Winnie is good with a triton—"

I stopped him midsentence.

"Mason, you're wasting my time. Go to bed. It's over; let it go," I said, disappointed.

"No, listen! We were going down the Risky River towards the Mermaid King, and Winnie told me something that's really important. She told me about this secret swimming hole her grandpa used to take her to and how they used to dive into the water from a huge oak tree."

"Yeah, so?" I said, wishing he would stop interrupting my sleep.

"Josey, the swimming hole is that little spot on the

map in area twenty-three. Plus, she said they used to dive in! That means the water—"

I finished his sentence, "—is really deep!"

Deep enough for huge walleyes, deep enough to hide the Lost City!

-25-

Friday morning's alarm couldn't go off soon enough. I was up early and anxious.

I had tossed and turned all night, dreaming about finding the Lost City. It seemed like I checked my cell phone every hour.

Finally, at 7:00 a.m., I jumped out of bed and went into Mason's room.

It was empty.

I walked towards the kitchen and then into the dining room. "Mason?" I yelled.

No response. I walked frantically through the house, but no one was there. I turned and went through the long hallway that connected the house to the bait shop.

As I neared the shop, I could hear loud talking. Puzzled, I opened the door to see a packed bait shop. Mom, Dad, and Mason were already waiting on customers.

I made eye contact with Mason. He looked at me then quickly away. I sensed something else was going on.

I walked over and whispered, "What's going on? Why so many customers this early?"

Mason ignored me at first. For some reason he was very reluctant to tell me what was going on. I asked him again, and this time, much louder and in a stern voice.

A customer across the counter intervened. "Didn't you hear? On the front page of the local paper, Winnie Moss confirmed the location of the Lost City!" he said.

My mouth dropped as I spun and glared at Mason. His head was down, and he was doing his best to keep working.

The customer held up a copy of the *Baudette Daily*

Newspaper. There on the front page, printed extra large and bold, read the headline:

Moss Reveals Location of the Lost City!

My blood boiled as I grabbed Mason by the arm and dragged him into the hallway.

Mason protested, "I don't know what's going on, Josey. Winnie and I played *Gauntlet* until 2:00 a.m. She never said anything. I woke up this morning to Mom getting me up to help with all the customers."

The news was out. It seemed like the whole state of Minnesota had headed through Baudette on their way to fish the Lost City.

I pushed Mason back into the house. "You need to call Winnie right now. I can't believe she betrayed us," I demanded.

"Ummm…I don't think I'm going to call her."

"Yes! Yes, you are, Mason! We need to talk to her right now!" I growled.

Mason just lifted his arm and pointed out the window of the bait shop.

He was right; he didn't need to call her. Her station wagon had just pulled into our driveway!

-26-

We rushed out the doorway and headed straight for Winnie, who was sitting in the car revving the engine.

"How could you?" I yelled as I opened the passenger door.

"Quit yapping and listen," she said. Her voice was firm but passionate. "Go grab the ice-fishing sled and load everything in the back. We're going back to area twenty-three, and I'm going to take you to my old swimming hole," she barked at us.

Mason and I took off for the garage and loaded the sled into Winnie's station wagon.

"Get in!" she ordered us.

"I have to tell my parents where we're going. I'll be

right back," I explained as I turned toward the house. I walked in through the back door to the kitchen.

The house was squeaky clean and decorated to the extreme for tonight's family Christmas party. Mom had spent the entire week getting ready.

"Mason and I are going to help Miss Moss today," I yelled out to Mom.

Mom was so distracted; she didn't even look up or acknowledge me, so I continued down the hallway to the bait shop. Dad was already swamped with customers, so I knew he would be looking for our help.

Mason and I are going to help Miss Moss today," I whispered to Dad from behind the counter.

He stopped his conversation and turned to me, excusing himself from the customer.

"Really? Winnie Moss? Honey, I need you and Mason. You know this is the last day of the Ice Queen and one of our busiest days," he exploded.

"Dad, I know, but she really needs us; she has no one," I replied.

Dad drew a deep breath and calmed down. "Go

ahead. I need to talk with you and your brother before the party. And you know Mom needs last- minute jobs done, so don't be gone all day," he pleaded, showing signs of a heavy heart.

"No problem. Dad, I love you," I said as I gave him a quick squeeze and a kiss on his cheek.

"I love you, honey," he replied and turned to his customers.

I quickly ran out the back door and jumped into the car.

I didn't even have time to ask; Winnie already knew what was on my mind.

As she quickly pulled away from the parking lot, she explained, "I didn't tell them about the swimming hole, but I didn't really lie. I called the editor of the paper and told him there are some anglers really close to the Lost City, and I think they might find it soon. When he asked me to be more specific, I remembered my grandpa talking a lot about fishing west of Pine Island."

Pine Island is one of a group of islands that

shelter the bay from the open waters of the Lake of the Woods. It's a well-known fishing hot spot, but after Winnie's latest revelation it seemed like every ice fisherman on the lake was moving all their gear towards Pine Island.

"It's called a smoke screen—a diversion. It will give us time to get back to number twenty-three's swimming hole. If that's where the Lost City is, we don't need any added attention."

She grinned. "Plus, like I said, *west* of Pine Island. Zippel Bay is west of Pine Island too."

And we went flying down the road, intent on one mission—find the Lost City to save our family business.

-27-

The Zippel Bay parking lot was once again empty. In the summer, the park was packed with families taking advantage of the beautiful beach. But this wasn't summer. The weather was much colder than the night before; it was snowing lightly again.

This time we didn't need the map since Winnie knew exactly where the swimming hole was. We walked about a quarter mile down the beach until we hit a small frozen stream extending onto the beach.

Winnie stopped and looked back towards our car. "This is it. I'm sure of it," she declared.

Looking around, it didn't look like much. The water, although frozen, was very shallow. That was not ideal for any fish, let alone walleye, and most definitely not the Ice Queen.

She led us down the frozen stream and into the woods. Several times we stopped, and she looked around and seemed confused. "I don't remember it being such a long walk," Winnie finally said.

*Great…*I thought. *Just what we needed.*

We walked on, ducked under dead trees, and jumped over dry spots where the stream stopped because it was too shallow to even freeze.

After about fifteen minutes of aimless walking, Winnie turned at us with a triumphant look on her face. "There, I told you!" she exclaimed, pointing down the stream.

About 100 yards in front of us, the water opened up to a hidden pond. It was big and looked like it was completely frozen over. There were no signs of any fishermen, let alone other humans.

"See that huge oak tree—that was our swinging tree. The deep water's right next to it," she confidently declared.

The pond itself was big, almost the size of a football field. It was abandoned, almost like time had forgotten it.

The three of us shuffled along the fresh snow and ice towards the middle of the pond, directly by the edge of the old oak tree.

"This spot looks as good as any place to start," I decided.

Mason unloaded the ice auger that was bigger than the one we had used yesterday, and it took the strength of both of us to hold it upright. He yanked on the rope, and the auger roared to life.

We firmly gripped it and pushed it into the ice. The auger was sharp, and within seconds, ice and snow were flying all over. We applied more pressure and hit something as our hole filled with a brown liquid.

"We hit dirt, still too shallow," Mason said.

We had only gotten down to the middle of the handle on the auger.

Winnie was walking around the perimeter of the pond while we headed out towards the middle of the pond. I told Mason to stay back as I took the ice spud ahead to check the thickness of the ice. To my surprise, the ice was really thick there, making it safe for us to proceed closer to the middle of the pond. My dad had always taught me to take ice safety very seriously.

"Might as well try here," I said after we had gone a ways.

The auger once again started shredding the ice and snow. But this time, instead of our seeing brown water fill the hole, cold, blue-colored water flowed up and onto the ice.

We had broken through the ice and hit water. We looked at each other with one question on our minds: *Is it deep enough?*

I took a scoop and got out the broken ice until we had a clear hole. Mason laid down on his belly, putting his face above the hole. "Looks deep! All I see is blue!"

"This could be it. Please let it be it!" I begged.

Mason started auguring as I pulled the sled over

and set up the fishing poles. We had four poles, each outfitted with a different color Swedish Pimple.

Mason put two holes about two feet apart so we could use the poles and jig in each one.

"Let me see how deep this place is first," I told him. I grabbed a pole and lowered the lure down, and it kept going and going. When I finally hit bottom, I figured the hole to be about at least 18-feet deep. "That's walleye deep!" I shouted.

After the lure hit the bottom, I started to reel it up, and then I felt something heavy and hard hit the line. I yanked and reeled until the lure finally broke free.

Attached to the hook was a large piece of wood about a foot long.

The wood was rough and weathered. It looked like some sort of wood siding—the same kind of siding that would have been used on an ice shanty many years ago.

We had just found the Lost City!

-28-

I had lost track of time. Our trip to the hidden pond and finding the deep hole had taken much longer than I would have thought. It was already late afternoon.

Winnie walked over and examined the piece of wood. She too was sure it was from a shanty. This spot was a hidden gem, especially for ice fishing.

Besides being a long walk and hard to find, the pond seemed locked away from the world.

Winnie had started a fire on the nearby shore. Mason and I walked over to warm up before fishing the deep hole.

Winnie collected and cleared more firewood to stoke the fire. I wasn't sure if it was excitement or the heat of the fire, but I was fully warmed up and ready to see what we could catch.

Mason stayed by the fire while I walked back across the pond towards the augured holes we had made in the middle. I grabbed a bucket and my fishing poles.

I started jigging with two Swedish pimples, one was coral-colored and the other was red. They glimmered in the water as I dropped them deeper and deeper.

It didn't take long.

The coral lure got a hit almost immediately, and I dropped the other pole onto the ice. Mason and Winnie came running over.

I could feel the weight of the fish as it tugged and fought while I pulled it closer and closer to the surface. I had been ice fishing plenty of times but couldn't remember the last time I was so excited about pulling one onto the ice.

The dark outline of the fish started to materialize from the outline of the light in the hole. I could see it now and my hopes were confirmed— walleye! Its marble gray eye and gorgeous coloring sparkled as I pulled it through the hole. The fish was nice-sized. Mason pulled out our fish scale, and it weighed in at 9.8 pounds. While it wasn't the Ice Queen, it proved that there was walleye in the secret pond.

Winnie and Mason quickly got their gear in the hole and sat on the buckets, jigging for the Ice Queen.

This place seemed perfect! The small stream we followed was too shallow for any big fish to travel in or out. My thought was the fish in this secret honey hole were old and big. Plus, The Twelve had been able to keep the spot hidden, making it even more intriguing. We spent the next couple of hours catching fish after fish—all good-sized walleyes. The biggest one we caught was a 15 pounder. It was the most amazing fishing I had ever seen.

Mason had continued to make new holes to fish from. Finally he looked at his phone and rushed over to where I was. He warned me, "Josey, it's 6:00 p.m. We have to be home for the Christmas party by 8:00. That means we only have an hour left to fish because it will take us an hour to pack up and get home from here."

Just then I felt a fish hit my lure. But something was different with this fish. The tip of my pole bent over, almost touching the ice.

Something was playing with my jig—something gigantic!

-29-

The weight of the fish was obvious and unmistakable. Winnie and Mason both rushed over when they saw the extreme bend in my pole. I finally was able to hit the rod and set the hook.

My mind started to play tricks with me. *Did I snag a log?* The fish seemed to be heavy and slow moving to the surface. It almost felt like it was dead weight.

As it got closer, I wondered if the weight of the fish was too much for my small pole.

Mason squatted down and peered into the water. He quickly sat up and had a look of fear and excitement on his face. "Jo…Josey…I saw the marble eye. It's a wa-wa-walleye, and it's enormous!" he stuttered with excitement.

I held tight and felt the fish trying to shake the lure. It must be close enough to the top of the hole to see our lantern light. Winnie hustled over to the sled and grabbed another lantern and the hand-held spud. Then she disappeared behind me. Mason wasn't much help as he sat mumbling and jabbering about how big the fish was.

Everything around me suddenly went silent. It was just me and the fish. I tried to block out all the added pressure surrounding this fish but couldn't. I began to tremble. It started in my legs and quickly traveled throughout my whole body.

"Stay the course, Josey! You can't lose this fish!" I told myself.

The small pole swayed and dipped as the fish got closer and closer to the surface. Suddenly I saw a splash of color, and the fish rolled in the hole. WOW! It was big—extremely big!

The fish dove back down towards deeper water and almost jerked me down with it. The line went tight and slammed against the edge of the augured hole. I gave the fish some slack on the line, and it raced back towards the bottom—towards the Lost City.

I wasn't going to let that happen. I quickly tightened the line and started bringing the giant back to the surface.

After a couple minutes, I had the giant back in sight from the top of my hole. I almost had her to the surface. Mason tried reaching down and grabbing her by the head but couldn't; she slipped out of his grasp. She was tired, and I was too.

I mustered all my remaining energy and pulled the pole high in the sky, standing up on my bucket.

The weight of the fish was almost too much. The fish jerked to the right, causing the line to rub hard against the jaded ice.

Within seconds the line broke. The fish was gone.

-30-

I jumped off the bucket and dove towards the hole. The ice-cold lake water hit my arm and instantly numbed it. My hand hit something hard, but it didn't feel like a fish.

I frantically looked up to see Winnie on her hands and knees, holding a large dip net. The whole time I had hooked the fish, she had used the ice spud to make another hole next to my hole.

She had used the hole she spudded to net the fish at the moment the line broke. I looked over to see a huge walleye in the dip net.

"Wow, I've never been so happy to see you!" I exclaimed to Winnie. The weight of the fish was wrenching her back, and her face was strained.

Mason ran over, and the two of them flipped the giant marble eye onto the ice.

But was it big enough?

"Let's weigh it and see if it's the next Ice Queen," Mason exclaimed.

"We ain't got time," shouted Winnie.

I glanced down at my watch and noticed it was almost 7:10 p.m. The Ice Queen Competition ended at 8:00 p.m., and no entries were accepted after the deadline.

"We got to go and fast!" I shouted.

I loaded the huge walleye into the sled as Mason and Winnie added the gear. Within minutes we were jogging back along the snowy stream to the beach, then straight down the beach to Winnie's station wagon.

"We aren't going to make it," I cried out as the car came into sight.

"Yes, we are; quit whining!" bellowed Winnie.

We made it to the car at 7:40 p.m. and rocketed down the road towards downtown Baudette. I couldn't help but stare at the walleye as I cradled it on my lap in the backseat. I wondered if this was a descendent of Augustus Moss' original Ice Queen.

How long had this fish hidden in waiting at the Lost City? I didn't believe in dumb luck or accidents. This fish was definitely a Christmas miracle, a gift of hope—not just to save our family's bait shop, but it had also connected us to Winnie.

That old station wagon sputtered and rumbled all the way to Main Street in downtown Baudette. The Ice Queen stage was next to the ice rink in the park.

The mayor was on stage at the podium counting down the last 45 seconds of the contest when I flopped the fish onto the stage. Gasps and whispers echoed through the town square, as people gathered closer to get a look at our fish.

My eyes darted to the leader board. There were some really big fish listed on it. Walter Lewis, a grizzled old fisherman, was currently in first place with a 17.3-pound walleye. With no other fish in sight but ours on the stage, the town bell rang, loudly signaling the end of the contest.

A hush fell over the crowd as the mayor placed our walleye on the scale. The pendulum teetered back and forth with its weight.

Time stood still. My eyes floated to the sky as a snowflake drifted down slowly. This holiday season was truly magical.

Mason tugged on my arm, bringing me back to reality.

"We won!" he exclaimed, jumping up and down.

-31-

"What?" I shrieked.

The crowd was going crazy, and I was having trouble hearing what the mayor was saying. I squinted through the lights and snow and read the scale. It showed 18.1 pounds!

"That can't be!" I said to Mason, out of breath. I quickly added, "It has to be bigger than 18.3 to be the Ice Queen." Tears started to form in my eyes.

"Josey, we still won $10,000!" cried Mason. He was dancing and acting like we had won the lottery.

The mayor called us up onto the stage and handed us an awkward huge cardboard check as we smiled for the newspaper. After taking several pictures, he leaned in. "Here is the real check.

Don't spend it all in one spot!" he advised with a wink as he handed me the check. I quickly zipped it in the side pocket of my winter coat. We thanked him as he turned to leave.

I scanned the crowd and the stage.

"Mason, where's Winnie?" I asked.

"Not sure, she left as soon as we took off running for the stage. She said she had something important to do, probably went home to play *Gauntlet*," Mason replied.

I wanted to thank her; we could have never caught this fish without her. I glanced down at my watch and saw that our Christmas party had already started. It was 8:05 p.m., and I was sure our parents were freaking out because we were late.

"Mason, we have to go now! We're late and have to tell Dad the bad news. We didn't get enough money to save Baxter's Bait shop. Grab the walleye; let's run," I ordered him.

Then it registered with Mason. His jubilant spirit seemed to deflate. While we won, we hadn't caught the Ice Queen. Our $10,000 first place prize would have made any other kid feel rich but not us. We felt like we had lost it all. We came close but had to have around $17,000 to save the shop. We were $7,000 short.

We turned and starting running for home. I guess we looked pretty funny running down Main Street holding a huge walleye. We made it to our house only ten minutes late to the party.

Cars lined the street, and our driveway was flooded with people. We quickly darted up the back porch steps, leaving the walleye outside in the snow.

We burst through the door and were greeted with hugs and attention from our family who had been waiting for us.

I was politely trying to make my way over to Dad. I wanted to be the one to tell him about the fish and the $10,000. But I couldn't get through all the people fast enough. I grimaced when I heard my dad's voice.

He cleared his throat and began, "Now that Josey and Mason have decided to join us, I have something to share with you. And I know it's not good news."

The whole family grew silent, giving Dad all their attention.

-32-

"I need to let you know that Baxter's Bait Shop has closed its doors today," Dad shared in a thick, choked-up voice.

Gasps could be heard as the Christmas music played in the background. Someone walked over and shut it off.

"Of course it is, Dad, for this year! It's our family's two-week vacation. Merry Christmas and Ice Queen," I yelled as everyone cheered.

I tried to make it sound like we were closing shop until the new year.

"Dad!" I shouted.

Dad looked in my direction defeated. I had hoped there was some way to still save the shop. In my heart, I just wasn't ready for Dad to make the announcement.

"We won the Ice Queen contest! Mason and I won!" I said waving the $10,000 check around in the air like a flag.

The crowd of family cheered even louder. Dad and I met in the middle of the room and hugged.

"You did what? How? When? Where?" he asked, his eyes opening wide.

"Dad, it's a long story, but here is a check for $10,000. I know it's not enough, though, but I was hoping you had some money saved up too," I said sadly.

"Honey, don't you say that. What you and Mason did for our family is more important than any bait shop. You did your best, and you did it for the love of your family."

"I know, Dad, but it's still not enough to save the shop," I said with defeat.

"I didn't know you knew," he said as he pulled me in for one of his famous Dad hugs.

"I overheard you when Mr. Hathaway stopped into the shop."

We worked our way across the crowded room giving high fives. In my mind, I wasn't sure why everyone was celebrating. It was awesome to win, but we fell short of saving the bait shop. The family that had gathered were totally fooled by the announcement that we were the first Baxters to ever win the Ice Queen contest.

Finally, we met Mason and Mom in the kitchen. Mom was teary-eyed, and Mason had his head down.

"Now you stop that. We all did our best. But we owe too much money, and we're still short. I need to make the announcement to the rest of the family," Dad said.

"Dad? The bait shop?" Mason asked, trying not to cry.

"I know, son, I know. But we'll be fine; we'll just figure something else out," declared Dad, reaching out with his big arms around us all.

The party was still going strong. Loud Christmas music, eggnog, and crazy Christmas sweaters filled our house, along with hope and excitement. But not in the kitchen, the harsh reality of losing the bait shop was sinking in as sadness and defeat surrounded us.

After a couple minutes of silence, Dad spoke up. "Okay, Baxter family, there's a rocking Christmas party going on at our house. We need to enjoy it and be thankful for all the family who are healthy and here to celebrate this year."

He walked over to the counter and grabbed his worn and tattered Bible. It was an annual tradition that Dad always shared the Christmas story found in the book of Luke.

"Let's not forget the reason for the Christmas season," he said, smiling genuinely. After a quick hug, we wiped our eyes, trying to make it look like we weren't crying and headed to rejoin the party.

I was the last to leave the kitchen. Suddenly, I heard a knock on the back door. At first I ignored it, but whoever it was just knocked louder. I let go of my mom's hand, as she nodded and headed into the living room. Mom smiled and began greeting everyone along with Dad and Mason.

I went over to the back door and opened it. The cold air took my breath away as I looked around, but no one was there. I glanced down and noticed fresh footprints in the snow.

There was a small, wrapped present sitting on the steps to our house. I bent down, picked it up, and started walking back to the warmth of the house.

I set it on the counter and turned to join the rest of the family in the living room. But something inside me told me to stop and open the package. I picked it up and inspected it. The package was wrapped with perfection in metallic-red paper with a bright, green bow.

I opened it and couldn't believe my eyes. It was loaded with cash—much more money than I had ever seen.

I quickly counted it. There was exactly $7,000 with a small note that read:

*Guess who won the **Gauntlet***
Winter Blast Tournament?!
Merry Christmas and Happy Ice Queen!
– icequeen56623

About the Author

LANE WALKER is an award-winning author, speaker and educator. His book collection, Hometown Hunters, won a Bronze Medal at the Moonbeam Awards for Best Kids Series. In the fall of 2020, Lane launched another series called The Fishing Chronicles. Lane is an accomplished outdoor writer in the state of Michigan. He has been writing for the past 20 years and has over 250 articles professionally published. Walker has a real passion for outdoor recruitment and getting kids excited about reading. He is a former fifth gr ade te acher an d el ementary school principal. Currently, he is a Director/Principal at a technical center in Michigan. Walker is married with four, amazing children.

Find out more about the author at
www.lanewalker.com.